MOTHERHOOD

SIAMAK VAKILI

ISBN
978-1-961601-31-4 (Paperback)
978-1-961601-32-1 (eBook)

MOTHERHOOD

The fragrant cool breeze of early spring blew aside the lace curtain of Dr. Mitra Shahverdi's bedroom window on the second floor of her apartment on Karim Khan street in *Shiraz*[1], further opened the ajar window and slowly hit it to the side of the television.

It was midnight and Ms. Shahverdi who had been tossing and turning but still could not sleep, felt a pleasant tremble go up her spine as she felt the cool midnight breeze on the bare skin of her arm. She pulled up her thin blanket up to her neck and filled her lungs with the inviting fragrance of the spring breeze and once again closed the eyes that were opened by the soft hit of the window to the side of the television and tried to sleep.

The next day was March 20th 1982 and the day the old year would give its place to the new one. Therefore, her seven day holiday and rest would start from the next day. And she was smiling with closed eyes as though she was going over all this in her head. But suddenly and exactly at that moment, she heard something fall and her apartment slightly shook. Ms. Shahverdi jumped up in fear, sat up in her bed and in the midnight silence and the dim light of the moon stayed alert, dazed and motionless. She did not know from where the sound had come or whether it was from hers or a neighbor's apartment. A few moments later, assuming that the sound had come from the neighbor's apartment and that perhaps she had just imagined it, she became calm enough to lie down once again but she suddenly heard a

---

[1] A city in the southwest part of Iran.

sound like a murmur, a moan or maybe a whimper of a child that was coming from the bathroom. She silently tiptoed toward the bathroom and put her ear to the door. No! She was not wrong; a blend of sobbing and moaning of a child could be heard from the other side of the door.

Ms. Shahverdi looked around to see if she could find anything to defend herself with; she did not find anything. So trying hard not to make any sound, she tiptoed away and went to the kitchen, slowly took out a big kitchen knife from the drawer and came back in the same manner. She once again stood behind the bathroom door and started to listen; she heard the same sobbing and moaning. Therefore, while squeezing the knife handle in her hand and holding its blade in front of her, she gently opened the door and with an extraordinary speed turned the light on. Suddenly and to her amazement, she saw a scared naked little boy who was sitting in the bathtub crying. The kitchen knife fell off the trembling hands of Ms. Shahverdi on to the bathroom tiles, making a ringing sound, and without blinking, she stared at the little boy with her astonished and confused eyes.

****

The little boy seemed to be around five or six and could hardly be seen among the thin velvet blanket that Ms. Shahverdi had wrapped him in, and now with scared eyes he was looking at Ms. Shahverdi and the police lieutenant who both were standing still and staring at him as if he were a space alien.

A few minutes passed until the lieutenant finally broke his silence, turned to Ms. Shahverdi and said:

"Maybe he doesn't understand what we're saying…I mean he doesn't speak Farsi."

"What difference does it make?"

Ms. Shahverdi said this and in response to the lieutenant's puzzled look added:

"I mean…you probably have certain people down in the police station that know other languages. So there won't be a problem. Isn't that so?"

The lieutenant who had all along been standing still in front of the boy, for the first time slightly moved and turned to Ms. Shahverdi while saying:

"That's true. But that won't change anything."

Then, from the corner of his eye, he glanced at the boy and continued:

"Tomorrow is *Nowruz*[2], everyone has gone on holiday and except for a few special agents no one else is in the station. So there's really nothing we can do during these days."

Ms. Shahverdi gazed at him and said:

"What? What in the world am I supposed to do with this kid who I don't even know nor have any idea where he has come from? I don't even speak his language!"

---

[2]   The Persian New Year.

"Maybe he is deaf."

The lieutenant said this and with a somewhat reflective look, stared at the little boy. Ms. Shahverdi asked:

"What difference would that make?"

"Well, if he is deaf then at least he knows sign language and so you can make him understand certain things by the use of signs." Ms. Shahverdi who was shocked said:

"You must be joking."

"No, not at all! Being deaf is far better than not understanding each other's language."

"Forgive me Sergeant…"

"Forgive me, lieutenant!"

"Forgive me, lieutenant! As you can see I'm a single woman and I can't take care of him by myself."

The lieutenant raised one of his eyebrows and said:

"Forgive me for saying this, but you speak of this kid as if you're referring to a dangerous wild beast."

"That's not what I meant…"

"In any case, Ms. you're the one who has found this kid and until the offices open again, taking care of him is going to be your responsibility."

Ms. Shahverdi guffawed and said:

"What in the world…? I haven't found this kid! He came out of nowhere and I don't know how!"

"Doctor! I've been doing this job for twenty years but I have never heard or seen anybody falling naked from the ceiling."

"I've already told you…and you have already investigated and seen it for yourself; all the doors and the windows were closed from inside, except for the bedroom window on the second floor and the outside wall is covered with marble…even a cockroach would slip on it!"

The lieutenant who had already begun to slowly back down while Ms. Shahverdi was speaking, hearing that she has finished, slowly turned and while walking toward the door said:

"In any case, whether you're the one who has found this child or he's the one who has found you, we won't be able to do anything until the holidays are over."

Ms. Shahverdi with a sudden leap reached the hall and stood in front of the lieutenant and said:

"I won't let you leave unless you take him with you!"

The lieutenant traced Ms. Shahverdi's pointing finger to where the little boy was sitting, took a look at him and again turned to the doctor and said:

"Take him with me where?"

"How should I know? Take him to your home!"

"That would be against the law ma'am. He'll have to stay with *you* until the holidays are over and the law decides his fate."

"What about the police station? Can't you take him there?"

"Oh yeah…we could do that! We could get him down to the station and leave him in the hands of bunch of lowlife dangerous criminals who don't even have mercy on their own mothers. You're a doctor…you are educated… do you think this is the right thing to do?"

Ms. Shahverdi who was intensely angry and irritated up until then, suddenly became calm and while looking at the child, in a whisper—while one could detect a tone of doubt in her voice—asked:

"So what would you do if you found this child on the street?"

The lieutenant immediately answered:

"We would hand him over to the child protective services until his case is cleared up. And that would need a court order but since everywhere including the court is closed, this child must stay with you until the end of the holidays."

And he turned to face the corridor that would take him out of the apartment. Dr. Shahverdi once again took a big step and stood in front of him:

"Tell me, Sergeant…"

"Lieutenant!"

"Forgive me, lieutenant! Tell me…if you yourself found this child on this very day that everywhere is closed, what would you do with him?"

"That's quite obvious! I would take him with me to my house and would take care of him until the offices reopen."

"Well, you could do that now. Why won't you take him with you?"

"That's because you're the one who has found him and you're the one who's responsible for him and therefore should take care of him."

Then while heading toward the front door he added:

"You have my number. Call me if you need anything… I'll be at your service. Goodbye!"

Ms. Shahverdi watched him disappear down the corridor and hearing the door close, she slowly turned and faced the little boy, stared into his small shining eyes and noticed that the signs of the initial anxiety and fear could no longer be seen in them. She sat in front of him and looked at him all wrapped up to his cheeks in the blanket. After some time, she suddenly asked:

"Are you hungry?"

The little boy nodded.

"You're hungry?

"Yes!"

Ms. Shahverdi got up to go to the kitchen but suddenly stood still in the doorway, slowly turned and once again stared into his small shining eyes.

Ms. Shahverdi stayed awake all through the night and not taking her eyes off the little boy's small face—sleeping on the sofa wrapped in the blanket—smoked until the next morning. Therefore, when the boy woke up in the smoke-filled room, his first reactions were fighting for breath and heavy coughs. Without saying a word, the doctor half opened a window and once again sat before the kid. The little boy sat up on the sofa, rubbed his eyes with his small hands and in response to Ms. Shahverdi's gazing eyes, stared at her. Finally the doctor gave up and while lighting up another cigarette asked:

"Don't you want to wash up?"

The boy nodded.

"Well the bathroom is right over there."

Ms. Shahverdi said this and pointed to bathroom and since the boy did not make a move, she added:

"There's a towel there too."

The little boy still did not move and kept staring at her. Ms. Shahverdi asked:

"Didn't you say you wanted to wash up?"

The little boy nodded again.

"So why won't you move?"

"I've got nothing on. How can I go to the bathroom?"

Ms. Shahverdi whose face was hidden among a thin cloud of smoke, said:

"If you're such a chatterbox then why were you mute last night?"

"That policeman was here too."

"Yes he was, but policemen are not scary. *I* asked him to come here."

"You wanted him to take me away."

"First of all don't address me as 'you'. And secondly… yes, I wanted him to take you to the police station."

"Why?"

"Because then they could find your parents."

The boy immediately answered:

"But I don't have any parents."

Ms. Shahverdi looked at him in silence for a while and then asked:

"Are they dead?"

"I don't know…I don't remember. Maybe I never had any parents."

"How can that be? Everyone has parents."

"So how come I don't have any?"

The doctor was once again silent. Then, as she was lighting up another cigarette, she said:

"You do too. Everyone does. How can anyone not have any parents?"

And after she took a puff on her cigarette, she continued:

"That's why I asked that police officer to take you to the police station so that he could find your parents."

She then gave the little boy a bed sheet and said:

"Here! Wrap this around so that you could go to the bathroom. I'll go look to see if I can find something for you to wear."

The little boy wrapped the bed sheet around himself and while going to the bathroom, he said:

"But I know that I don't have any parents."

"Do not repeat that again."

Ms. Shahverdi said this and instantly asked:

"By the way, what's your name?"

The little boy turned to her but stayed silent. The doctor said:

"You don't have a name either?"

"I don't know…I don't remember."

After thinking a bit, he added:

"You see? I don't have any parents. If I had any then I would have a name too!"

And he went into the bathroom. While he was gone, Ms. Shahverdi tried to prepare a breakfast that consisted of bread, cheese and hot sweet tea and when she heard the bathroom door close, she shouted:

"Come to the kitchen and eat your breakfast."

The little boy walked into the kitchen and without saying a word sat at the table and began to eat. The doctor, while leaning on the kitchen counter and smoking, looked at the clock and then turned her face to the window. Every day, at the very hour, meaning seven thirty in the morning, she could hear the outside commotion that signified the start of life and work, but that day was silent and calm everywhere. Dr. Shahverdi slowly reached the window and beyond the lace curtain took a look at the alley and then at the street; only a few from that everyday bustling crowd could be seen here and there and a car sometimes passed through the street. She once again walked back to the kitchen counter to put her cigarette out and looked at the little boy from the corner of her eye. Taking no notice of his surrounding, he was slowly and patiently eating his breakfast. Ms. Shahverdi poured herself some tea in a narrow waist tea glass. She put the glass on the counter and while folding her arms, she stared at the little boy with a seemingly contemplating look and finally asked:

"How can I call you if you don't have a name?"

The little boy raised his head and looked into her eyes but did not say anything.

"How would you like me to call you?"

The little boy still said nothing. He looked as if he had not understood her question. Ms. Shahverdi took her tea, put it on the kitchen table and sat on the chair. She said:

"I don't get it! How did you get into the bathroom last night? All the doors were closed, how did you get in?"

The little boy kept looking at her with a mouth full of bread and still did not say anything.

"Why were you naked? Where are you clothes?"

The little boy still did not utter a word. Suddenly Ms. Shahverdi's voice exploded like a grenade:

"Who are you? Where have you come from? Why aren't you saying anything?"

She then slammed her hand on the table and hastily went out of the kitchen. She then entered the living room, angrily dropped herself on the sofa and muttered under her breath:

"Damn it! Damn this luck of mine! What a holiday! It's like I can never free myself from the curse of misery."

She then furiously threw the cushion to the wall and pressing her teeth together in a muffled voice shouted:

"Where did this rascal come from? Where did it come from?"

She then lay on the sofa, closed her eyes and with a few deep breaths tried to regain her calm.

A moment later, feeling numb all over, Ms. Shahverdi took a short nap but then she thought she heard the little boys' voice. She opened her eyes and listened to his voice; she could hear the little boy crying in the kitchen. She kept her eyes half open and tried to give in to the pleasant numbness and sleep again but the broken whimpers of the little boy started to disturb her. Annoyed and frustrated, she finally got up and went to the kitchen. The little boy was squatting under the table, holding his legs with his arms and resting his head on his knees. Eyebrows crossed and biting the corner of her lower lip, Dr. Shahverdi looked at the little boy who was hardly visible among the blanket for a while and finally asked:

"What are you crying for?"

The little boy immediately and with the same whimpers answered:

"It's none of your business!"

Not expecting to hear such an answer, the doctor angrily said:

"It's none of my…? You should behave yourself! Besides, this is my house and your cries won't let me sleep."

"So I'll leave."

He said this while still crying and then instantly added:

"You wanted to hit me!"

"What…? I never waned to hit you!"

"Didn't you hit you hand on the table?"

Ms. Shahverdi paused a bit and then with a voice which she was trying to keep calm said:

"Well, I was stressed out, but…"

"That's just it! When that happens, mommy's hit their kids."

"I'm not your mother!"

The little boy shouted:

"And I don't you to be either!"

And after a series of continuous whimpers, the little boy suddenly broke into a loud cry. The doctor who was shocked, in order to calm him down said:

"I didn't mean anything by that…I meant someone else is your mommy…"

But as if he has not heard what she said, among his loud cries, the little boy again shouted:

"And I'm not your son either! Get it? I'm not your son either!"

Arms folded and leaning on the door frame, Ms. Shahverdi who was still standing in the kitchen doorway and biting her lower lip, crossed her eyebrows and while tapping her right foot with a steady beat on the floor, stared at the little boy with a contemplating and desperate look, but it seemed that the boy was not going to calm down.

Sighing out of resentment and desperation, Ms. Shahverdi finally went back to the living room. She dropped herself on the sofa and turned on the T.V; some people were sitting around the *Haft-Seen*[3] table and were talking about *Nowruz*, *Haft-Seen* and such things. She

---

[3]   Haft-Seen or the seven S's is the traditional table setting of Nowruz.

listened to them for a bit. Then she turned down the T.V, picked up her cell phone, found Gity's number and called her. The instant she heard Gity's voice, she said:

"There's a 5 year old kid in my house."

Gity burst into laughter and said:

"Naughty girl! Why were you hiding it all this time?"

"I'm not in the mood for jokes Gity. This kid has suddenly dropped from the sky and I don't know what to do with him!"

"Whose kid is it?"

"It told you I don't know…I found him last night in the bath tub…all naked."

"Where has he come from?"

"You're not listening to me! I told you I don't know… he himself doesn't know. All the doors and the windows were closed. I heard a sound from the bathroom and when I went there I saw him scared and naked in the tub. The police doesn't know anything either. I can't take him anywhere since everywhere is closed. So I'll have to take care of him for the remainder of the holidays, but I don't know how?"

"What are you talking about?"

Gity said this in amazement. Ms. Shahverdi went on saying:

"I don't know…I mean, this is just my bad luck. This morning I asked him where and how he had come here. He says he doesn't know anything. It looks like a temporary amnesia. However, since he was not saying anything and was silently staring at me with his big black eyes, I got irritated and hit my hand on the table. Ever since, he's been continuously whining like a kitten and telling me all sorts of things. He says I wanted to hit him."

"That's how kids are…"

Ms. Shahverdi combed back her hair with her hand and said:

"You know how much I hate kids and their whining! I'm going mad…can you come over?"

"Today? And at this hour? Are you crazy? The new year's about to begin and I can't go anywhere! Besides, you know that leaving your home and family on the eve of the New Year would bring you bad luck…"

Ms. Shahverdi immediately asked:

"Will you ever stop? Don't you ever want to quit believing in such nonsense and superstitions? What do you mean it brings you bad luck?"

"Not everyone's like you, your highness! You think you're living in a research laboratory and everything must proceed according to science and its laws. And then on days like this that are supposed to be the happiest ones of all, you stay all alone…"

"But in my opinion such days are the best time to rest, to have some peace and to read a book…"

"Mitra! Living outside of the laboratory means the very same rituals, customs and the very same superstitions…"

Ms. Shahverdi with a lifeless and seemingly impatient tone said:

"All right! Stop lecturing me, will you? Just tell me what I should do with this elf and how I can shut him up?"

Gity laughed loudly and said:

"I have never thought you could put Mitra and a kid next to each other…"

"Gity…what should I do with him?"

"All right, all right! Talk to him, give him candy and nuts, read him a story…hug and caress him…"

She then shouted:

"Iraj! Can't you see the kids are jumping up and down on the table?

Then with a calm and a bit hurried tone, she added:

"Mitra! The kids are messing up the *Haft-Seen*. Call me again if you have any problems…kiss you!"

And she hung up. Dr. Shahverdi also threw her phone on the sofa and while letting out a long-winded sigh through her inflated cheeks and half open mouth, combed back her hair with both hands and feeling confused and irritated threw herself back on the sofa and said in a whisper:

"Hug and caress him…!"

She then threw her head on the cushion with a sudden move and stared at the ceiling. She could still hear the whimpers of the little boy. She listened to them for a while and tried to put on a clam face. Then, with long steady steps she went to the kitchen. Wrapped in his blanket, the little boy was still crying and whining. Ms. Shahverdi squatted down and for a while looked at the little boy who was clearly trying to draw some attention. Then with a seemingly appeasing tone she said:

"All right…that's enough!…I…I'm sorry…what I did was not right. I shouldn't have lost my temper and hit my hand on the table."

And she waited for a while. The little boy ignored her and continued to cry even louder.

"I said I'm sorry…"

And since the little boy still ignored her, she added:

"Fine…I'll say it again; I'm sorry! Did you hear me? Did you hear what I said kid?"

The little boy for the first time since he started to cry, raised his head from his knees and with a wet and dirty face looked at her and said:

"I'm not a kid!"

Ms. Shahverdi looked at him a little. She said:

"Very well! Now come out from under the table boy!"

"I'm not a boy either!"

Ms. Shahverdi seemed very tired but she could not help laughing and said:

"Then what are you? A girl?"

The little boy shook his head.

"So you're a man then, huh?"

The little boy nodded yes. Ms. Shahverdi said:

So what should I call you then? Little man?"

Then while still laughing, she added:

"Or maybe *mister*? Oh, I know! How about if I call you young man? Huh?"

Seeing that the boy's face was slowly lighting up, she added:

"…that's it; young man! It suits you fine…you're young and a man. Isn't that so?"

She then winked with her big black eyes at the little boy and made him laugh joyfully. Then, while trying to look and sound playful, she added:

"Now if you come out of there and wash up good and be a good young man, we'll go out together and before the shops close I'll buy you some clothes, candy and nuts. You do like candy and nuts, right?"

The boy nodded and immediately came out from under the table and stood before her. Ms. Shahverdi said:

"Very good! Now go wash up while I dress up!"

The little boy went to the bathroom with a cheerful smiling face and when he came out with the same look and all wrapped in a blanket that was being dragged behind him, he saw that Ms. Shahverdi was ready. The doctor took a look at him and at the blanket. She then took a pair of scissors, cut the extra part of the blanket and with it wiped dry the little boy's face. Then, she put a pair of slippers in front of his feet, and the little boy without hesitating shoved his small bare feet into them and started to flip-flop behind her.

It had rained that morning and so the air was cooler than a typical spring day and it smelled of wet dirt and damp sprouts. The few people that could be seen on the streets were hastily passing by and except for the vendors who were trying to sell something in those last hours of the year, there were no open shops. After an hour long search in the streets, Ms. Shahverdi and the little boy finally bought what they needed from the very same street vendors and returned home.

The little boy put on his new clothes the instant he arrived home and with a happy face looked at himself in the mirror. Without changing, the doctor dropped herself on the sofa and watched the little boy who was now cheerfully opening up the packs of candy and nuts. Then, she took off her head scarf, threw it into a corner, ran her hands through her hair and with a rather anxious tone said:

"Be careful not to throw any on the floor!"

The little boy took a look at her and got busy again. The doctor turned the T.V on and got up to take off her coat. The people who were sitting around the *Haft-Seen* table were still busy talking. The boy went near the T.V and stood in front of it. Ms. Shahverdi went toward her room, glanced at the boy and said:

"Don't sit so close to the television! Sit on the sofa if you want to watch it!"

And she entered her room. While taking off her coat, she heard the little boy saying:

"It's the *Haft-Seen*! Why don't we have any?"

"Because we don't have any…"

Ms. Shahverdi said this while coming out of her room, buttoning up her skirt and pulling up its zipper; she added:

"Didn't I tell you not to sit so close to the T.V?"

"Why?"

"You'll hurt your eyes…"

"No…why don't we have a *Haft-Seen*?"

Dr. Shahverdi looked at the little boy's small face and felt that he would probably start to cry again. She said:

"Nothing to it! We can set up our own *Haft-Seen* in a flash!"

"It'll be too late!"

"No! We still have time, as you can see."

And she pointed at the television. Then, while taking the packs of sweets and nuts to the kitchen, she asked:

"Do you know what things we must put on the *Haft-Seen* table?

"Anything that starts with *S*…"

The little boy said this and while running after her to the kitchen repeated:

"Anything that starts with *S*."

Ms. Shahverdi raised her eyebrows and said:

"Bravo! Who did you learn that from?"

Seeing that the boy had only become happy with her praise but was not answering, she asked:

"Did you learn it from your mom?

The boy nodded yes.

"Maybe your father has taught you that?"

The little boy once again nodded his head. Ms. Shahverdi looked at his happy face and big black eyes with a comforting smile and after a moment said:

"Now do you know why they should start with *S*?"

The little boy nodded his head but did not say anything.

"Well…because it's *Haft-Seen*…"

The little boy nodded again and Ms. Shahverdi added:

"Therefore, we can also put a *soosk*[4] on the table?"

And she looked at him with a mischievous grin and added:

"*Soosk* starts with S…"

"Euugh…"

He said this laughingly and added:

"But *soosk* is dirty…"

"You mean if it weren't dirty we could put it on the table?"

The boy swung around joyfully and said:

"No…*soosk* is dirty. It's ugly too. It always comes out at night…"

---

4   Soosk means cockroach in Persian.

"Too bad! So we can't use a *soosk*, since it's almost New Year and it's not dark enough for us to find a very big one…otherwise, we could give it a nice bath until it was all clean and pretty, then we could towel dry it and then put it on the table next to the sweets…"

The little boy gave himself a joyful twist and acting disgusted said laughingly:

"Euugh…then it'll eat the sweets…"

Ms. Shahverdi, whose face had slowly lit up with the joy of seeing the boy's happiness, while going round the kitchen table to open one of the cabinets, said:

"So we'll let you hold it in your arms…you could take care of it then. Then it will crawl up your shirt and get in through your collar…"

She said this while tickling him under his chin and added:

"It's both warm and cozy in there…it will love it…"

The little boy burst into fits of giggles and tried to pull up his collar to stop her from tickling him.

He then managed to escape her and with the same laughter ran to the living room but then almost instantly came back and with a quick move took a cookie and started to run out again. Ms. Shahverdi ran after him to give him a plate and said:

"Put it in here and be careful not to drop any crumbs on the floor."

The little boy took the plate and kept running. Ms. Shahverdi watched him run out and started to take out and count some plates from the cabinets. She then placed all the S's in them and with a never seen before care, she decorated them. Then, she leaned on the edge of the sink and calmly looked at them.

"How many years has it been since the last time I did such things?

She asked herself this question as if she was whispering out her thoughts. Then, with the tips of her fingers she wiped and dried the corners of her eyes and then shouted:

"Come over here…hurry up! Hurry!"

The boy came quickly and with his smiling face looked at her and the plates that were laid on the table.

"Where are you young man? Help me take the *Haft-Seen* to the living room."

Trying to keep her face cheerful and childlike, Ms. Shahverdi gave one of the plates to the little boy and added:

"Put it on the table in the living room."

And when the boy was taking the plate, she said:

"But be careful not to drop it."

The boy left the kitchen with slow steady steps and Ms. Shahverdi followed him with a tray that had the rest of the plates in it. They laid the plates on the table and lit a candle among them. Then, they put a flower pot next to them along with the sweets and the nuts. Ms. Shahverdi poured a glass of sour cherry *sharbat*[5]—that she liked very much and her mother had sent her—and put it in front of the little boy and for herself, and poured some black tea in a narrow waist tea glass that had a golden rim. She then sat on the sofa, lit a cigarette and looked at the boy who was still standing close to the television. She said:

"I told you not to sit so close to the T.V…you'll ruin your eyes…come sit here on the sofa."

Without saying anything, the little boy turned around and sat next to her on the sofa and watched her smoke her cigarette. Ms. Shahverdi tried to escape his stare; she put out her cigarette and noticed that there's only one cigarette butt in the ashtray. A faint smile was formed on the right side of her lips as she peered into it. She took her glass and passed a glance at the little boy who was still watching her. Before putting the sugar cube into her mouth, she asked; "You still don't remember from where and how you came to be here?"

The boy shook his head:

"Nope!"

"How about your mom and dad? Do you remember them?

"Nope!"

"So you don't remember your name either?"

"Nope!"

---

[5]   A traditional Iranian fruit-flavored drink which is served chilled.

The little boy said this last *nope* with a smiling face and so tenderly that the doctor laughed involuntarily and gave him a pat on the head. The boy's face became merrier than before. He stood on the sofa and leaned back. He said:

"Why do we have to set a *Haft-Seen* table?"

"It's a tradition."

"What does that mean?"

"That means we always do this. Anything that is always done is a tradition."

"Why?"

"Why what?"

"Why is it a tradition?"

Ms. Shahverdi whose face had become prettier with her clam and kind smile, lit another cigarette and said:

"Well, this dates back to thousands of years…to the time when Iranians believed in different angels that they called *izad*. Like *izad* of water, *izad* of rain, *izad* of land… they believed that…"

"What does *izad* mean?"

"I told you already…it means angel! They used to call the angels that were close to God *izad*. The *izads*…"

The little boy slowly slid down the sofa and while keeping his eyes fixed on her mouth leaned against her knee. Ms. Shahverdi took a look at him with a smiling face and while trying to move aside the drooping hair on his forehead, went on saying:

"…each one was a guardian of one the most important blessings of God. One…"

The little boy, little by little, pulled himself up, sat on Ms. Shahverdi's lap and stuck himself to her chest. Ms. Shahverdi felt that his warmth instantly ran through her body and made her shiver all over. She then felt a burning sensation in the depth of her nose and then the slight wetness in the corners of her eyes. She put her cigarette on the ashtray and continued:

"…one was the guardian of water, one was the guardian of earth and so on. They called them *Amshasepand. Sepand* means holy. A flower or a plant was named after each of these *Sepands* and every year at the time of New Year, just like now, they used to put these flowers and plants on the *Haft-Seen* table and they called it the seven S's, meaning the seven *Sepands*. These S's are the first letters of the *Sepands* which means holy. Along with them, they used to put *sharbat*, sweets, nuts, fruits and everything else that they had. Of course, they used to put the gold fish and their holy book as well. It used to be the *Avesta*[6] but now it's mostly the Quran. They also place *Divan-e-Hafez*[7] on the table…"

"What about colored eggs?"

The little boy asked this with a stretched tone while he was playing with Ms. Shahverdi's shirt and stared questioningly into her eyes.

---

[6]   The holy book of the Zoroastrians.

[7]   A book of poetry written by Hafez, the 14th century Iranian poet.

"You're right! We almost forgot about the most important thing…then how could we play with eggs in the New Year?"

The little boy's face split into a wide smile and looked at Ms. Shahverdi's hand that was rubbing the tip of his nose with her index finger.

Ms. Shahverdi who had slowly forgotten the situation she was in, moved a bit and suddenly realized that she had wrapped her arms around the small body of the boy and was tightly squeezing him. She said:

"Oh…we have forgotten about *Divan-e-Hafez*…"

And while putting down the little boy from her arms, she added:

"Sit here till I find it."

She then quickly went to her bedroom, closed the door behind her and sat on her bed. She could hardly breathe and when she covered her face with the palm of her hands she could feel her burning hot skin. She got up and sat at her makeup table, stared at her rosy cheeks in the mirror and saw how her eyes involuntarily were filled with tears.

The sound of Nowruz horns and drums were heard from outside her room. Ms. Shahverdi quickly wiped her eyes dry and went out. The little boy was once again standing in front of the television. The doctor sat on the sofa and lit a cigarette. Hearing the sound of the lighter, the little boy turned around and having seen her, ran toward the sofa, climbed up and stood on it.

"Do you know what this horn and drum sound means?"

Ms. Shahverdi asked this and the little boy instantly shook his head no.

"It means that we have just entered a new year…"

She then ruffled up his hair with the tips of her fingers and added:

"So happy new year! I wish you a great year and I hope you'll remember your parents soon and return to them…"

The little boy immediately jumped down from the sofa, ran toward her and held his arms up. Ms. Shahverdi did not at first understand the little boy and slowly bent down in bewilderment…the little boy wrapped his arms around her neck, kissed her cheek and while sticking out his tongue through his lips that were pressed against each other, buried his head in her chest and giggled. Once again, blood rushed in Ms. Shahverdi's face, her body heated up and was covered with cold sweat;

her eyes were once again filled with tears. Not wanting the little boy to see her face, she turned away and got up. She said:

"Do you want me to read you one of Hafez's *ghazals*[8]?"

And without waiting for the little boy's response, she went to her bedroom and after a moment came back with a copy of *Divan-e-Hafez* and sat in the same place. She said:

"Well? Concentrate on a wish!"

---

[8]   A short lyric poem written in couplets using a single rhyme.

Seeing his puzzled face, she added:

"That means you should make a wish…"

She looked at him a bit and then asked:

"Well?…did you make one?"

From the little boy's face one could tell that he had not understood anything but he nodded anyway. Ms. Shahverdi closed her eyes and while softly tapping her finger on the book, she whispered:

"O *Hafez* of *Shiraz*[9], you are the keeper of every secret…For the love of your *Shakh-e-Nabat*[10], tell us the secret of this young man's heart and tell us if his wish will come true or not."

She then opened her eyes and took a glance at the boy who was looking at her with a smile on his face and a question in his eyes and opened the book:

"Wow! What a beautiful ghazal! It says: *"No other lover like me is there in the land of the Magi…I have pawned my cloak in a place, my wine and my notes somewhere else…"*

She then read the whole ghazal, turned to the little boy and said:

This ghazal shows that this year is going to be a great year for you and some of your best wishes will come true."

She started to go through the book of poems. The little boy slowly came forward, leaned against her legs and stared at her trembling lips that were silently reading

[9]   Hafez was born in the city of Shiraz in Iran.

[10]   According to legends, *Shakh-e Nabat* was a beautiful girl to whom some of Hafez's poems are addressed.

the ghazals of Hafez. Ms. Shahverdi looked at his eyes, once again stretched out to touch his hair but quickly withdrew. The little boy asked:

"Are the guests going to come now?"

"Guests?"

"To visit us…"

"I don't think anyone is going to visit us today. We don't have anywhere to go to either."

She closed the book, got up and looked out the window:

"The weather is rainy too. Even if it weren't, we still couldn't go anywhere."

Then, she returned to her seat. She said:

"Today is the first day of Nowruz and everywhere is closed. No one is outside either."

"So what are we going to do?"

The little boy said this and slowly pulled himself up and sat in her lap. Trying to stop him from leaning against her chest, Ms. Shahverdi tried to pull herself back. She replied:

"I don't know!"

But the little boy kept looking at him with his puzzled face. The doctor asked:

"Why aren't you having any sweets or nuts?"

"I had some!"

"Have some more!"

"Don't want anymore…can't we go out?"

"Where to?"

"Somewhere…anywhere…"

Ms. Shahverdi took a long sigh and moved aside the hair on his forehead with the tips of her fingers. She said:

"Not today! But maybe tomorrow…"

She was about to touch the little boy's hair again but suddenly and slightly nervously put him down from her lap and asked:

"Do you like cartoons?"

With the same laughter and joyful twist, the little boy nodded yes. Ms. Shahverdi changed the station to a cartoon channel and said:

"All right…sit here and watch your cartoon…I'm going to take a bath. Don't get up from your seat and don't touch anything, okaay…?"

The boy nodded and stared at the television. When Ms. Shahverdi came out of the bath, she realized that the little boy was feeling drowsy and kept on moving around on the sofa. The instant he saw her, he moaned:

"I'm hungry…"

Ms. Shahverdi suddenly got worried. She approached him, knelt down before him, put her hand on his cheeks and forehead and even checked his pulse. She said:

"Why aren't you wearing your sweater?"

The little boy rubbed his eyes with the back of his hands and in the same dull stretched tone said:

"I was hot…"

"You're not hot…you're catching a cold. Come…"

Ms. Shahverdi said this and headed to the kitchen but the little boy stretched his arms toward her and stared at her with his sleepy, blurry eyes. Ms. Shahverdi took a glance at his now half closed eyes and softly took his hand, helped him down the sofa and took him to the kitchen. She helped him sit at the table, dissolved a powder in a cup of water and held it in front of his mouth. The little boy did not want to have it and tried to push it away.

"It's good for you. It will stop your cold and fever."

Ms. Shahverdi said this and also added:

"You don't want to get sick and force me to give you an injection, do you?"

The little boy drank up the whole potion and he frowned with disgust at its bad taste. Ms. Shahverdi poured tea in the same cup and added some rock candy to it. She mixed it with a spoon and once again held it in front of his mouth:

"This is will change the bad taste in your mouth."

The little boy drank half of the cup and pushed it away. Ms. Shahverdi once again put his hand on his cheeks and forehead and took his pulse. She said:

"All right! Now what do you want to have for dinner?"

Seeing that the boy is silent, she added:

"Do you like *Ghormeh Sabzi* [11]?"

The little boy nodded.

---

[11]   A traditional Iranian dish made with herbs, lamb and kidney beans.

"All right! If you help me, it will be ready soon…have you ever cooked *Ghormeh Sabzi*?"

The boy slowly shook his head from side to side.

"Really!? How can a young man of your age not know how to cook *Ghormeh Sabzi*?"

The little boy faintly and sleepily smiled.

"Well…first we'll soak the herbs, and cook the beans in boiling water. So while one is getting soaked the other will be cooked. We will then cut the meat into small pieces and fry them…do you remember now?"

While still showing weakness, the boy nodded yes with the same vague smile.

The next morning, at around ten o'clock, Ms. Shahverdi was sitting in a chair and having a cigarette while watching the little boy sleeping on the sofa. The ashtray next to her was filled with cigarette buds; it seemed like she had been awake and smoking all night. When the little boy got up, his first reaction was a few coughs. Ms. Shahverdi with pale and lifeless eyes that had been watching the little boy all night long, got up and opened the window to change the air of the room. The little boy sat up on the sofa with half closed eyes and pushed aside his blanket. While walking back to her seat, Ms. Shahverdi looked at the boy in order to tell him something; maybe to ask him to hurry and wash up as his breakfast was already prepared. But she froze half way and for a moment, with wide open eyes that were suddenly very worried, stared at the little boy whose face was chalk white, his lips were dry and his face was soaked in sweat and it seemed as though he could not keep his eyes open. She opened his eyes with her fingers and looked at their pupils and once again put her hand on his forehead. She said:

"You have fever…"

She ran to the kitchen to fetch the thermometer form the medicine cabinet. When she came back she saw the little boy spread out on the sofa, keeping his eyes open with difficulty, while clinging to his blanket with his small fists and trying to breathe…but he could not and his breathing sounded like a saw that was cutting a piece of wood in half. Ms. Shahverdi quickly ran to him, made him sit up and opened his mouth. Then with his index finger she pushed his tongue downward so that she could see into his throat. After that, using her thumbs, she gently applied pressure on both sides of his throat…she once again opened his eyes and carefully looked into them. She said:

"What's wrong? Why can't you breathe?"

The little boy was inhaling and exhaling with difficulty.

"Do you have asthma?…"

And because the little boy could not say anything, she continued:

"You have asthma…these are all signs of asthma… you didn't have asthma…did you?…I think you have asthma…no…I'm sure you have asthma…"

And while saying all this, she picked up the little boy and quickly left the house.

An hour later, Ms. Shahverdi came back while she was carrying the little boy whose head was resting on her shoulder. She closed the front door, set him slowly down on the sofa, took an asthma inhaler and a few canisters out of her bag and put them in front of him on the table. Then, she placed her hand on his face and forehead. She said:

"Your fever is lower. You're getting better but you're still sweating a bit."

She pointed at the inhaler and the canisters and said:

"You must have these on you at all times. Did you know that you had asthma?"

The little boy shook his head.

"And till now, you've been short of breath?…"

The little boy shook his head again.

"Very well! You should know that you have asthma. You must not run or do anything to become breathless. Do you understand?…And in case you do run out of breath, just like today, you hold this in front of your mouth and press this button. Do you understand?… like this…then you take a deep breath to inhale the gas that comes out of the canister…got it?…you hold it like this and press this button here…like this…did you get it?…"

The boy nodded yes every time. Finally, Ms. Shahverdi stopped asking questions and while looking straight into his big black eyes, she tossed aside the hair on his forehead, held his small face in her hands and felt his hot damp skin on the palm of his hands. She asked:

"Are you feeling better now?"

The little boy nodded again.

"All right! Now lie down and rest till I bring your breakfast."

Then, she brought him some tea, milk, cookies, bread and cheese and put them in front of him. Ms. Shahverdi sat near the little boy and watched him have his breakfast slowly. She even lit a cigarette once but immediately put it out. She also tried to keep herself busy watching television but her attention was constantly drawn to the little boy. At last, the instant the little boy finished his breakfast, she picked up the tray and headed toward the kitchen and while doing so, she said:

"Now lie down a bit and watch cartoon till I make you a delicious soup…I'll make it for both of us…okay?"

And she did not wait to see him nod and hastily went to the kitchen. Ms. Shahverdi put the pot of soup on the stove to simmer, returned to the living room and found the little boy asleep. She pulled the blanket over him and turned the television off. She knelt near the sofa, looked at his peaceful face and for a moment listened to his regular breathing. She touched his hair, his hot and damp skin until the image of the little boy started to wave and was slowly drowned in her tears. So she wiped her eyes with the back of her hand and went to her bedroom. She sat on the bed, embraced her legs and rested her forehead on her knees. After a few minutes, she raised her head and stared at the small shelf that was on top of her closet. Tears kept welding up and she kept wiping them off with the back of her hand. The skin of her face constantly got warm and rosy and was wrinkled with a deep sorrow. She finally got up, went to the shelf and looked at a small box that was in the right corner of it and under a few shoe boxes and some other things. Then, she sat back on the bed and stared at that box.

An hour later, she heard a sound from the living room. When she quickly went out of the room she saw the little boy trying to use his inhaler but did not know how. She took it out of his hands and helped him with it. When the little boy calmed down, he wrapped his arms around her neck and pressed himself against her. Ms. Shahverdi did not move at first. Then, she put her hands on his hot, wet back and felt that her whole being was heated up with the warmth of the little boy's trembling body. A pleasant feeling ran in her veins. She felt a burning sensation in her nose and eyes and her mouth and throat dried up. She gently pressed him against her chest and realized that her shivering hands were not strong enough. She wanted to lay him down on the sofa but he did not want to let go of her. She put her lips close to the little boy's ears and whispered:

"Don't be scared…I'm here…I won't go anywhere. You must lie down because you have a little fever. I'll stay here with you…"

And she could clearly see that the trembling in his body had subsided and his grip was loosened. She quickly but gently laid him on the sofa. She said:

"Get some sleep! You must rest. I'll wake you up when your soup is ready…okaay?"

Then she pulled the blanket up to his neck. The little boy kept looking into her eyes until his eyelids fell closed and his breathing became regular again. Ms. Shahverdi got up from his side as though she had been glued to the ground. She stood over his head for a moment and watched his small face that was still rosy and damp. Then she took her cigarettes and ashtray and went to the kitchen. She checked on the soup, opened the window, pulled up a chair near it, sat down and lit a cigarette.

A soft wind was blowing outside, rubbing the young branches of the trees against each other. The air was colder than yesterday and the rain that has been falling for the past hour was being drawn to the window panes by the wind. Sitting next to the half open window, once in a while, rain drops fell on Ms. Shahverdi's face and hands which made her close her eyes as she softly trembled all over. Her lips and cheeks were quivering and from the corners of her eyes a narrow stream was coursing down the sides of her nose and after passing her lips and her half open mouth, it was dripping down from her chin. The wind blew strong for a moment and opened the window wide. Ms. Shahverdi bent over and pulled the window to the way it was, then, she slowly pulled up her legs, embraced her knees and while shaking like a leaf, she bit her lower lip, pressed her eyelids together and suddenly started to sob; a soft sob…like the hiccups of a child.

After about an hour when she suddenly heard the boy coughing, Ms. Shahverdi came to herself and quickly ran to the living room. She stood next to the kitchen door that was near the living room; the little boy was coiled under the blanket and the moment his sleepy eyes caught sight of her, a big smile covered his whole face and he rubbed his eyes with the back of his hands. Seeing his happy face, Ms. Shahverdi gently smiled as well. She sat next to him and while tossing aside his hair that was wet and sticky with the fever sweat from his forehead, she asked:

"How's our young man feeling today?…"

Once again the little boy smiled. Ms. Shahverdi placed the back of her hand on his cheeks and forehead and added:

"Your fever has gone down…did you sleep well?"

The little boy nodded his head and tried to sit up.

"Are you hungry?…"

The boy nodded again.

"Our soup is ready. Sit right here and I'll bring you some…and put the blanket over your shoulders! Your fever has just gone down…"

Then, she threw the blanket over his shoulders herself and tidied up around him. She then went to the kitchen and returned with a bowl of soup which she put in front of him. She said:

"Blow on it first so you won't burn your tongue…"

Then, without noticing her own smiling face, she sat in her favorite armchair and watched the little boy eat. The little boy ate his soup with great appetite and drank his orange juice.

"Do you want me to bring you some more?"

The boy nodded and drank up the orange juice to the last drop. Ms. Shahverdi brought another bowl of soup and a glass of orange juice, put it in front of the little boy and as she was about to sit down again—still wearing her happy smile—she noticed the blinking light of the answering machine. She pressed its button and heard Gity's voice:

"Hello doctor…happy new year! I hope that this year brings you lots of happiness and smiles. Iraj and the kids send their love too and wish you a happy *Nowruz*. By the way, how's our little guest doing?…What did you do with him?…Call me when you get this…kiss…Gity!"

The message was left when they had gone to the drugstore—as the date and time matched. Ms. Shahverdi listened to the message with an almost blank face and turned on the television on her way back to her seat. Over images of flowers, blossoms, birds and rivers, a singer was singing a ghazal by *Rumi* [12]: "*What did you drink last*

______

[12]   13th-century Persian poet, theologian, and Sufi mystic.

night, tell me, do not hide…do not look at the sky like the innocent and the silenced…last night you poured wine and ran away from our sight…I have caught you again, do not do so again…" While immersed in watching the little boy, she listened deeply to the song. Suddenly a lightening struck and lit up the dusky sky and following that a thunder roared and it was so very sudden that the little boy immediately went to Ms. Shahverdi, pulled up his trembling body from her legs and sank in her arms. Ms. Shahverdi was more shocked by the little boy's behavior than the thunder; the little boy was curled up in her arms like a scared lonely kitten and having scratched her hand, he was staring at the window with his big black eyes— that were looking even bigger at that instant— and was breathing heavily.

The little boy pressed himself against Ms. Shahverdi's chest; so much so that his trembling body sent a shiver through her body which awakened a pleasant feeling in her…she felt warm inside, the sudden rush of blood turned her face crimson and her skin was soaked in a joyful sweat. She wrapped her arms around the little boy's small curled up body and pressed him against her. She said:

"Hushshsh…Hushshsh…it's okay…it's just a small thunder…nothing to be scared of…I'm right here…!"

The instant she uttered the last sentence, her eyes suddenly started to sting and were filled with tears…a cry was trapped in her throat and made her lips and chin quiver. She put her red hot face on the sticky hair of the little boy and with a slow and sorrowful tone repeated:

"…I'm right here…I'm right here…I'm right here…"

After an hour or so, she felt that the little boy's body had become loosened and heavy. She looked down at his face and eyes. He had fallen asleep. Trying hard not to wake him up, she got up and laid him on the sofa, pulled up the blanket all the way to his neck and tidied up the cushions around him. Once again she rubbed her hands on her damp sticky hair and checked his temperature by putting the back of her hand on her forehead. Then, she stretched out and yawned. It was past eleven at night when she looked at the clock. She whispered to herself:

"Today went by so quickly!…"

She took a long look at the boy. She could not read anything from his face. She looked around and then threw the tissue she had wiped her eyes with in the trash basket. Then, she went to the bathroom, brushed her teeth like a robot and looked at herself in the mirror as though she was seeing a stranger who she thought she had known in a very distant past. She did not finish brushing and left her unwashed toothbrush in the holder and came out of the bathroom. Then, she turned all the lights off except for a small night lamp on the television table. She went to her bedroom and left the door ajar to able to see the sofa the little boy was sleeping on. She sat on the bed and fluffed up her pillow a bit but did not go to sleep;

once again, she pulled her knees close, rested her chin on them, stared at the small box on the top shelf of her closet and gently rocked herself like a cradle.

Around midnight, she woke up startled by a loud thunder that shook the doors and windows of the house and found herself sitting with her knees still pressed against her chest and she instantly heard the terrified voice of the little boy—he had run into her bedroom with his eyes still heavy with sleep— which was a mixture of him crying, moaning and saying 'mommy' over and over again, and noticed him trying to pull himself up the bed. Still semi-conscious, Ms. Shahverdi threw his hands under the little boy's arms who was still crying and was repeatedly saying 'mommy' and greedily and quickly embraced him. The little boy was panting like a scared, wounded pigeon and was trying to cling on to her with his claws so as not to slip and fall.

"Huush…huush…huush…don't be scared…it's nothing…I'm right here….it's just a thunder, that's all… nothing to be afraid of…"

And she suddenly realized that her body is burning like a furnace and was shaking like a leaf and the voice of the little boy saying 'mommy'—which he had stopped saying—was echoing in her head. The more she heard this voice the more she lost control and with a passion that she had never experienced before, she constantly moved around her hands on the small, curled up body of the little boy and pressed him against herself so hard as if she wanted to suck in that whole small, trembling body and become one with it. Her red, hot and moist face was covered with a silent smile and at times looked like a cry and filled the springs of her eyes with tears that watered the flower-filled orchard of her face, lest it would grow yellow and dry up; and all because of one word; a word that still repeated in her head and had taken over her. However, no matter how hard she tried, she still could not utter the word herself. Her mouth was dried and sticky and had difficulty breathing. But she was not willing to exchange that moment with getting a fresh breath, until little by little that passion and excitement simmered down and peace returned to both their bodies and the little boy could finally raise his head from her chest, hold his chin up and look into her eyes. Ms. Shahverdi ardently gazed into his eyes, caressed his head and suddenly and involuntarily kissed his cheek and said:

"You're not afraid anymore, are you?"

She quickly said this and when the boy shook his head, she asked:

"Do you want some orange juice?"

And did not wait for him to answer…still holding him in her arms, she got up, went with him to the kitchen, poured two glasses of orange juice and while sipping them, they returned to the bedroom. But before entering the room, the little boy, with a stretched tone asked:

"Can I sleep with you tonight?...I don't want to be alone..."

Ms. Shahverdi's nostrils flared and as if a proud joy had come over her by this request, she replied:

"Only if you drink up your whole orange juice!"

The little boy nodded his head so happily that his cheek hit Ms. Shahverdi's shoulder and then he drank her orange juice to the last drop and held the empty glass in front of her. Ms. Shahverdi put the little boy and the empty glass on the table in the room and cleaned his face with a tissue. She then laid him on the bed and pulled the blanket over him. The little boy, who was lying behind her, slowly came nearer until his body touched hers. Then, he was relaxed and closed his eyes. While resting her head on her right arm, the doctor played with his hair and looked at his face...but once again she started to look at the top shelf while her eyes were fixed on the small box. Then, after a long while and without noticing whether the little boy is asleep or not, she asked in a whisper:

"Do you want me to tell you a story?"

She said this and without taking her eyes off the box, in the same whisper, continued:

"Once upon a time, there was a seventeen year old girl whose biggest wish in world was to become a doctor and to be called a doctor by all. But her family was so poor that she could barely finish her high school. The poor girl was constantly looking for a way for her wish to come true and was planning to work with all she had after she graduates from high school, to pay for her university fees. This had become a great nightmare for her; a nightmare that she could never escape from…not even when her wish finally came true! But one day, she met a man in one of her friends' homes…a man who she got married with a few months later. He was twenty seven years old, was majoring in physics and was going to get his Ph.D. in one year's time. He was not a bad man…actually he was a very kind and wise man and provided a comfortable and peaceful life for the girl. However, the girl who did not hate him and even liked him a bit, had only married him because she was poor and was planning to study with his money and thought that she would deal with anything else later in the future. Therefore, very soon she entered the School of Medicine at the University of Tehran. Everything was going as she had planned and the girl was about to change that horrifying nightmare into a beautiful reality…but one day she found out she was pregnant. Her nightmare suddenly came back and she decided to have an abortion. But her family and that of her husband's gathered around, did not allow her to do this and forced her to keep the baby. And finally, the day came when the baby was born; it was a boy!"

That joy was once again gone from her face. It seemed as though she was no longer noticing the little boy next to her. All that was left of her whole being were two eyes that were only seeing that box. She went on whispering:

"Finally, she could not take it any longer and six months after the birth of her child, she left him and her husband and never went back. She became alone and cut off her ties from the world, from her family and friends and even from herself! She studied in solitude, became a doctor and went to another town to live in without leaving a trace…there she tried to start a new, independent life; a life that she had always been dreaming of since she was a student in high school…"

While still gently playing with the little boy's hair, she looked at him intently and continued:

"…she thought it was too soon; too soon to get married, too soon to have a child. But damn poverty…that's what forced the girl to give in to all that. That little fairy who had graduated from high school with good grades, all for the love of studying in a university, did not deserve to lose her dreams like that…did she deserve it!?"

She looked at the little boy's face as though he was all ears and was listening to her story. She went on:

"…However, the girl never imagined that having a dream is very different from fulfilling it. She thought that in this way she could reach her goal and open the door of a lovely and fabulous life, but she did not know that she had actually closed all the doors in her life…"

Then while slowly getting up to fetch that small box, she said:

"…there are some things you can keep your distance from…as much as you want to…but you can never separate from them or even forget them…"

Holding the box with both hands, he sat on the bed next to the little boy, put it on her lap and while gently caressing his hair, he rubbed the top of the box and said:

"…many years passed for the girl to realize that many of the things that we see and want to throw away and get rid of for good are actually within us; they are us. We can keep our distance from them but we cannot throw them away…"

Then, as if she was talking to someone, she added:

"Look!…he must be about your age now…look!"

And a silent cry choked her throat…so much so that she could barely hear her own voice. But she was still trying to finish her words. Her words were like the panting of a bird after a long flight:

"…do you see how my heart is beating?…How I'm running out of breath?…How I sweat all over and burn inside?…look!…"

And her face wrinkled with a cry and once again the springs of her eyes started to boil. She went out of the room and gently closed the door behind her, sat on the floor, next to the sofa, put that box in front of her and stared at it.

After looking at it for a while, she opened it; there was only a photograph in the box. She took it out and looked at it. A woman was sitting on a hospital bed while holding a baby in her arms. His arm around her neck, a man was sitting next to her. On both sides of the bed, there were some other people who seemed to be their families. Everyone was smiling, except for that woman whose face was blank and lifeless. A sorrowful smile formed on her face as she rubbed her hand on the photo and her index finger on the small face of the baby.

When the little boy opened his eyes, the morning sun was shining its light from the only small window of the room onto the bed. He rolled from side to side and with his eyes that were still sleepy, looked for Ms. Shahverdi. He did not see her, so he rubbed his eyes with the back of his hands and slid down from the bed. He pushed open the ajar door and saw her sitting on the floor and holding a small wooden box on her lap while her left hand was resting on the sofa. She stood in the doorway and looked at her with the same sleepy eyes. With a pale face and tired eyes, Ms. Shahverdi, looked at him and gently smiled. She said:

"Hello young man…you have gotten up?"

The boy nodded with a smiling face and curled up next to her like a spoiled cat. Ms. Shahverdi, who was used to it by now, moved aside the hair on his forehead and said:

"Don't you want to wash up and brush your teeth?"

The little boy nodded and tried to stand on her lap.

"So…go brush your teeth and wash up until I prepare the breakfast, okaay?"

The little boy ran to the bathroom and Ms. Shahverdi, although still reluctant to let go of the small box, got up, put the box on the television, rubbed his hand on it once more and while going to the kitchen, took a glance at her cellphone and then at the clock; it was fifteen to seven. Once again, she looked at her cellphone and then went to the kitchen.

While having breakfast, Ms. Shahverdi watched the little boy and with a contemplating and eager look monitored his every move; she involuntarily watched him not to spill anything on his clothes, or not to take too big a bite and hold his tea glass with two hands and not to burn his tongue. The little boy did what she asked him to do and therefore evoked an unexpected excitement and a pleasant passion in her. There was no longer any trace of the stubbornness, rigidity and the *nope* saying attitude. Ms. Shahverdi's eyes were shining and by her calm, composed and tolerant behavior— which she had been showing for the past couple of days, especially on that second day of *Nowruz*—one could tell that a brand new inner disposition was about to be born; or actually, it had already been born and was gradually taking shape and maturing. She then looked at the sticky, ruffled hair of the little boy for a while and said:

"You have sweated so much in the past couple of days that your whole body is dirty and sticky. Do you want to take a dip in the bathtub?"

She said this with such a happy face that the little boy laughed cheerfully, although he did not reply.

"You *do* know how to swim, right? You're not going to drown, are you?"

Giving his body a joyful twist, the little boy giggled and raised his eyebrows.

"So while I fill up the bathtub with hot water, you can take off your clothes…or maybe it's better you take them off there…you might catch a cold out here!"

Then, she went to the bathroom and the little boy followed her while trying to unbutton his shirt. The doctor filled up the bathtub and helped him take his clothes off. When she was holding the little boy's hand and helping him get into the bathtub, she saw a not very old wound on the inner part of his arm. She held his arm up and examined it; a small part of his skin was gone. She asked:

"What has happened here?"

"Got burned with a hot frying pan…"

"A pan!?"

While nodding, the little boy twitched his lips and in a rather sad tone said:

"My sleeve got stuck when I wanted to take the fork out of the pan…it was so hot."

Ms. Shahverdi looked into the little boy's eyes reflectively and said:

"When did it happen?"

"I don't know…last year…"

"It couldn't be last year! This is a very fresh wound…"

She then gently rubbed the wound with her thumb, examined it once more and then said:

"Maybe two or three months ago…"

Then, once again she looked into his eyes and asked:

"Tell me…you remember how you got burned but you don't remember your mom and dad!?

"I don't know…"

The little boy said this with a serious look and added:

"There's one here too…look!"

And he showed the palm of his left hand where exactly below the thumb, one could see the scar of a healed wound that was as small as the point of a needle. Ms. Shahverdi took his hand, rubbed her thumb over it and looked at him from above her eyes.

"It happened in kindergarten. I fell down and a nail went into my hand…

The little boy said this and then spread his arms wide and said:

"It was this big…so big…"

And then he suddenly added excitedly:

"The playground is so big…you can never reach the end of it…not even if you run forever!"

Then as if trying to remember it again, he repeated:

"It's so big…"

And he tried to finish his sentence. Ms. Shahverdi asked:

"Do you know where it is?"

The little boy was about to nod but then suddenly he shook his head from side to side and then stared at Ms. Shahverdi. The doctor looked into his eyes for a bit and then said:

"Very well! We'll talk about it after your bath. Now sit down…slowly…slowly…don't slip now…watch out! It's slippery…can you look after yourself?"

And after the little boy nodded joyfully, she added:

"I didn't fill it too high, so that you could play around."

Then, with a bath jug she poured water on his head and washed it with shampoo a couple of times. She then said:

"Okay! Now stay a bit more in the water and play until I come back later to wash you up."

And she went out of the bathroom.

It was almost ten o'clock. The sound of the little boy playing in the bathtub could be heard and she was still sitting, looking at her cell phone and playing with her pack of cigarettes. She had not smoked for the past twenty four hours and it seemed that she was not craving for any either. It was then when she suddenly got up and picked up her cell phone. She pressed it in her hand for a bit and then found a number and dialed it. The skin of her face was red and burning and there was a hazy veil before her eyes.

The number she had dialed reached an answering machine and the voices of a man and a child were heard:

"Hi! We're not home, so please leave your message and we'll see what we can do!"

She hung up her cell phone and pressed it against her chest with joy and a smile on her face. She got up and walked around the living room. She dialed the number again and listened to their voices with a childlike excitement.

It was past two in the afternoon. The little boy had already come out of the bathroom and was watching cartoon and perhaps for the twentieth time, Ms. Shahverdi was dialing the number, listening to the voices on the answering machine and laughing joyfully. The little boy looked at her at times, smiled with her, despite not knowing the reason for her joyous laughter.

Finally, Ms. Shahverdi found another number from her phonebook and hesitantly dialed it. A middle aged woman answered from the other end of the line. Once again, feeling hot and sweaty all over, Ms. Shahverdi said in a trembling voice:

"Mom!"

There was silence on the other end but the sound of her anxious breathing could be heard.

"Mom! Hi mom, it's me, Mitra!"

"I know my dear! I know! How could I not recognize the voice of my own Mitra? I dreamed about you a few nights ago…I swear to God I dreamed about you. I knew I would hear from you soon…"

"Mom…Mom!"

"What is it my dear? Your voice is still the same…"

"Mom! I've been calling Behzad since morning, but all I get is the answering machine."

"They're not home, my dear…"

And she turned silent.

"Is that Behnam's voice on the answering machine?"

"Yes my daughter! Did you notice what a voice he's got? You should see how handsome he's become…"

"Where are they? Are they on a trip?"

"No! Nothing important…but his asthma…"

"Asthma? Does he have asthma too?"

Ms. Shahverdi said this so loudly and with such amazement that the little boy fearfully turned and looked at her with wide worried eyes. Ms. Shahverdi smiled at him and with a wave of hand asked him to calm down. While keeping an eye on him, with a voice that she was trying to keep calm and stress-free, she asked:

"He has asthma?"

"Yes! Since he was three years old…"

"Is he okay?"

"On the night before the new year, around midnight, he fell ill and Behzad took him to the hospital…"

"Hospital!?"

"It's nothing my dear! He's okay….his last canister had run out of medication in kindergarten and it had taken them too long to find him one…so he faints…"

but he's in the hospital now and Behzad is with him at all times…"

"What for?"

And because she sensed something terrible from her mother's silence, with a louder and nearly mournful tone, she repeated:

"What for? Why does he have to be in the hospital for two days for not getting a canister in time? Is he not feeling well?"

"He's in a coma!"

Her mother said this hastily as though she was getting something off her chest. And Ms. Shahverdi, with an excessive emphasis on the word 'coma', added:

"How can asthma make someone go into a coma?"

"I don't know my dear…but the doctors say that it's temporary and that he will wake up soon…"

"Which hospital?

"Tehranmehr! On the corner of Mirdamad and Naft Street…but it's nothing my dear…don't worry…"

"Do you have the number?"

"They're not home…"

"The hospital's number…do you have it?"

"I do…"

Ms. Shahverdi wrote down the phone number, hung up her phone and immediately called the hospital. Only when the receptionist picked up, did she realized that having panicked she had forgotten to get the room number. Therefore, she gave the name of Behzad Sassani, explained Behnam's illness and was finally put thorough to his room. When she heard Behzad's voice, Ms. Shahverdi was almost ready to burst into tears and felt that she had suddenly been thrown into an oven; she was burning like one who had a fever but her face was as white as fresh plaster. She listened to Behzad saying hello a few times but could not reply and hung up the phone.

The theme song of *Tom and Jerry* was echoing in the silence of the apartment and Ms. Shahverdi could hear her breathing and heartbeat among that familiar sound as she was squeezing the cell phone hard in her hand. She had placed her free hand in her hair and was breathing with difficulty. Feeling dizzy, she dropped herself on the sofa, shut her eyes and bit her lower lip so hard that a drop of blood rolled down from the corner of her mouth. A while later she got up and took a deep breath and sent the air down her lungs; like a person whose body is deteriorating from within with a lethal pain. Then, she went to the kitchen, took a bottle of water out of the refrigerator and desperately drank from it as though she had been thirsty for days. She dropped herself into the chair and tried to regain her calm. Then, she called the hospital again and hearing Behzad's voice, with a sound that seemed to being uttered through a swallowed cough in the throat, she said:

"Hi…"

She paused. It seemed she was waiting to hear a reply from Behzad, but since he remained silent she added:

"…this is Mitra…"

"Mitra!? Is that you, Mitra?"

"Yes…how are you?"

"Me!? Not bad…"

And he remained silent and amazed. Mitra hurriedly and still confusedly said:

"Mom told me that Behnam is not well…what happened? She said he is in a coma. Why? How's he feeling?"

In between her broken questions, Behzad replied:

"Because of his asthma…his inhaler ran out and by the time they get him a new canister, he faints. But he was better afterwards…I don't know why, but he was once again short of breath around midnight…and he went into coma before we could reach the hospital…"

"Why coma? Hasn't he woken up yet? Why coma?"

"I don't know…his doctor says that he's actually unconscious…because of lack of oxygen to his brain. It took some time to get him the new canister…"

And he turned silent and so did Mitra. It was as though they both had just realized one thing; why had Mitra called after so many years?

"I wanted to know how he was doing!"

Mitra said this slowly and hesitantly and hung up the phone without saying anything further.

The sound of *Tom and Jerry's* melody could not be heard anymore but one could hear the sound of the rain that had started to pour a few minutes before. While squeezing the cell phone in her hand, Mitra walked to the window and through the glass she watched the raindrops falling on the asphalt outside. The dust on the windows was being washed down by the rain and small crooked streams were now flowing down from the top of the glass. After looking at the window glass and the asphalt and listening to the sound of the pouring rain for quite some time, Mitra turned toward the corridor and when she reached the living room she saw the little boy trying to change the channel. She asked:

"Like to take a trip?"

"Where to?"

And he nodded yes at the same time.

"Tehran!"

The little boy laughed and after about ten to fifteen minutes he found himself standing in front of Mitra who was hastily buttoning up his pants and tying his shoelaces. Then, with the same haste and excitement, they got into the car and in the early spring air they drove to Tehran. Around five in the morning, Tehran was as crowded as it could be at any time of the day. It was as though, the city had not slept the night before. It was only five minutes past five when they reached the hospital. Mitra was holding the little boy's hand and was hurriedly pulling him along. She got the directions to Behnam's room and when she opened the door, Behzad had just woken up. The instant he saw Mitra, he ran toward her and pushed her out of the room. He said:

"What are you doing here?"

And closed the door.

"How is he?"

Behzad stared at her baffled and said:

"He's woken up…he woke up an hour or two after we spoke together…now he's feeling better, but…"

"So he's awake now!"

"Yes he is! But I asked you what you were doing here?"

"I've come to see Behnam!"

"He's not Behnam anymore…he's Poorya now!"

"You've changed his name?"

"I did it a few days after you left."

And he pulled her along with him to the end of the corridor, where a hot water dispenser was placed. He said:

"Now what is it that you want after so many years? Poorya has…"

"I don't want anything. What could I possibly want?"

"Then what is it? Poorya has gotten used to this life…"

"I just want to see him. That's all!"

"Don't you understand? There's no *you* and *I* anymore! Don't you remember when you left? You were supposed to be dead. What would he do if you showed yourself to him? What would *you* do after that? I've told him that you are dead…"

"I'm dead?"

"So you have forgotten everything! What else did you expect me to say? What should I have said in response to his countless different questions? That you left the instant you were born? She left because she was afraid of you?"

"That's not why I left…"

"Then what was the reason? Let us not repeat what happened five years ago; the same quarrels, the same words, the same pretensions, the same justifications…"

"I left because I was afraid of myself…"

She said this with such stifled cry that blood suddenly rushed through her face and her mouth and lips dried up. She added:

"…I didn't know what to do. I was still too young…I had plenty of time to study and achieve what I wanted instead of having to raise a child…"

"Well, now you have achieved it. What else do you want? You can't have your cake and eat it too! I don't understand why some people think raising a child is some sort of backwardness?

"Isn't it?"

"Is it? Then why have you come all this way, begging to see him? Is it? So look at me; do I look backward to you? Look at yourself; do you look progressed? Have you really ever looked at yourself? No friends, no acquaintances… you haven't even spoken to your parents in five years. You have left your own child to achieve *this*? And then you name it *progress*?"

"I know…I know, but I don't know what has happened to me in the past one or two days that I'm not the same Mitra that I used to be five years ago…what am I saying? I'm not even the Mitra that I used to be three days ago…"

She said all this with a hasty fervor and suddenly turned silent while staring into Behzad's eyes. Behzad looked at her face for a moment and said:

"Even if we could have and do what we wanted five years ago, today we can no longer do so. I don't think it's a good idea to show up like this and then just leave him with hundreds of unquestioned answers…"

"I will answer all his questions. I'm his mother…"

"His mother!?"

"He's my child…"

"Your child!? You must be joking!"

"No! I'm not joking…I myself don't believe that I could have such a feeling but he's my child and I'm his mother. I want to see him…I'm begging you. I don't want to leave him anymore…I want to stay with him…I want to…"

And suddenly the words broke in her throat, she fell down on her knees and while tightly clutching Behzad's pants she moaned so miserably that it made Behzad kneel down involuntarily and try to help her breathe.

"Please…I'm begging you…he's my child…he's my dearest thing…he's my everything…he's my life…he's my life…"

Mitra said all this with such a woeful moan that it was no different from the howl of a dying wolf. Behzad was kneeling next to her in bewilderment and was looking at the her hot wet face and her tearful eyes and witnessed how Mitra was gradually drowning in their boiling spring and her face was no longer visible. Finally, he grabbed her arm to help her stand up and then took her to Poorya's room.

When Mitra opened the door, she found Poorya awake with red sleepy eyes. She knelt down next to his bed and said:

"Hello…how are you feeling?"

"I'm fine!"

Poorya said this and looked at her smilingly. Mitra instantly put her hand on his cheeks and forehead and with a worried look, carefully studied his medical chart that was hanging at the end of the bed. Then, she returned toward him, knelt down again and took his pulse. She said:

"Everything is all right…you're all better…how do *you* feel? Do you feel any better?"

And while looking at his smiling eyes, she put his hand on her hot dewed face, rubbed it on her lips and kissed it. With the same cheerful smiling face, Poorya pulled his hand out of her hands and rubbed it against her cheeks. Mitra took a look at the palm of his hand and noticed a scar at the bottom his thumb. She held his hand close to her eyes and examined it carefully and just then she remembered the little boy. She looked back at the door and not seeing him she suddenly and quickly jumped up and while screaming out 'young man,' she ran toward the door but before looking out in the corridor she turned around and looked at Poorya who was still staring at her steadily and smilingly with a face that seemed anxiously curious and intense. So she held his small hand and gently rubbed her thumb on the small scar and with a doubtful and trembling tone asked:

"Do you know how you got this?"

Poorya nodded with the same smiling face and then said:

"I was playing in kindergarten and I fell down…"

And gradually smile faded from her face and her eyes darted from side to side, but before he could say anything further, suddenly as though she had just remembered something, Mitra pulled down her sleeve and saw a scar of a newly healed wound. For a while, she looked at it so intensely that it scared Behzad into almost pulling out

Poorya's hand out of her trembling hands, but just then Mitra asked in a scared hoarse tone:

"Did you burn yourself on a frying pan!?"

Poorya nodded, his face crinkled and his lips shivered but before he could say anything else, Mitra jumped toward the door and with a husky and whimpering voice cried out:

"Young man! Young man!"

And in a fearful haste, she ran through the corridor from side to side several times and her cries finally turned into a painful moan as she ran to the reception desk. She asked:

"Have you seen a little boy? He was about four or five years old and was wearing a red sweater…the boy who came along with me?"

And before waiting to get an answer, she ran toward the hospital exit, called out for the little boy and then returned. The man and the woman who were at the reception desk looked at each other and then at Mitra and a few people who were sitting in the hallway also stared at her. While clinging tightly to the ends of her manteau, she was still looking everywhere with her bulged out eyes and scared face that was wet with tears and finally after hopelessly calling out for the little boy from the depth of her throat with a hoarse and agonizing voice for the last time, she suddenly turned silent and ran toward Poorya's room. Behzad was standing in the middle of the corridor and did not know what was going on. When Mitra quickly passed by him, he asked:

"Who's this *young man*?"

But Mitra was standing in the doorway and was looking at Poorya. She slowly walked in, knelt down at his bedside and stared at this face. She asked:

"You do know who I am…don't you?"

Poorya nodded and smiled.

"You do know…you do know…"

Poorya once again nodded with the same smiling face.

"I'm here…I'm here with you…I will never let you go…never. Never young man!"

And she pressed his forehead against her chest and tried to swallow her sobs so as not to reveal her insane cries!

THE END

SIAMAK VAKILI